Sweet
Dreams!

To Stella, Luna,
Max, Paz, and You—
thanks for reading!
—G. S.

Sweet Dreams!

By Holly Anna • Illustrated by Genevieve Santos

LITTLE SIMON
New York London Toronto Sydney New Delhi

LITTLE SIMON

An imprint of Simon & Schuster Children's Publishing Division
1230 Avenue of the Americas, New York, New York 10020
First Little Simon paperback edition October 2020
Copyright © 2020 by Simon & Schuster, Inc.
Also available in a Little Simon hardcover edition.
All rights reserved, including the right of reproduction in whole or in part in any form.
LITTLE SIMON is a registered trademark of Simon & Schuster, Inc., and associated colophon is a trademark of Simon & Schuster, Inc.
For information about special discounts for bulk purchases, please contact Simon & Schuster Special Sales at 1-866-506-1949 or business@simonandschuster.com.
The Simon & Schuster Speakers Bureau can bring authors to your live event. For more information or to book an event contact the Simon & Schuster Speakers Bureau at 1-866-248-3049 or visit our website at www.simonspeakers.com.
Designed by Laura Roode
Manufactured in the United States of America 0920 MTN
2 4 6 8 10 9 7 5 3 1
This book has been cataloged with Library of Congress.
ISBN 978-1-5344-7835-0 (pbk)
ISBN 978-1-5344-7836-7 (hc)
ISBN 978-1-5344-7837-4 (eBook)

CONTENTS

☆ Chapter One ☆

The Magical Kitchen

I, Daisy Dreamer, am making *rainbow* popcorn in the World of Make-Believe. The WOM is my favorite place to be! And, by the way, the letters *WOM* stand for "World of Make-Believe." *Obviously.*

I'm in the kitchen with my *amazing* imaginary friend, Posey. We met each other at school one day when I drew a picture of him.

The next thing I knew, Posey *jumped* off the page and into my life, and things have been pretty magical ever since!

Speaking of magic, *everything* in Posey's kitchen is *unbelievable*. When I open the fridge, it plays a song—same

with the oven, the stove, and the dishwasher. Even the teapot whistles a happy tune! It's like being at a concert!

Posey's kitchen is beautiful, too. The cabinets are striped and swirled in pastel colors, and the floor is a pink-and-yellow checkerboard pattern.

I play hopscotch on the squares every time I move around. I mean, how can I not?

Then I hear a splashy sound. *Plink! Plunk! Plink! Plunk!*

It's Posey dropping dough into the mini doughnut machine. I can't wait to try one!

But first I have to finish making my rainbow popcorn. Plus, I have a batch of fizzy cupcakes in the oven. They are soft on the outside and fizzy on the inside! Yummers!

Posey and I sing and dance while we work. But I stop as soon as I realize something very silly.

I have no idea why we're baking all these goodies!

So I tap Posey on the shoulder and ask, "What are all the treats for, anyway?"

Posey tosses the mini doughnuts in the air and catches them all with his

antlers. Chocolate sprinkles tick onto the floor.

"You ask the most perfect questions, Daisy!" he says, wiping doughnut crumbs from his fur. "The goodies are for *tomorrow!*"

"Oh," I say, because that hardly seems like a clear answer. "What's so special about tomorrow?"

Posey throws his arms in the air. "Tomorrow is your very own Daisy DREAM DAY!"

My eyes grow wide because I want to know MORE.

"What's a Dream Day?" I ask.

Posey leaps onto the counter and spins in a circle. "A Dream Day is when the *whole* World of Make-Believe celebrates a human's imagination."

All at once Posey's words unlock *more* magic in the kitchen.

SWOOSH!

The oven door swings open—*all by itself*—and begins to play music. My fizzy cupcakes pop out of their pan and fly to the counter. Whoa!

We watch as the cupcakes are magically frosted and decorated. Finally they settle onto a plate.

That's when Posey and I are swept up into the air! *Wooo-hooo!* We swirl around the kitchen in a parade of dancing treats!

I squeal like crazy, because I *love* to fly!

Posey whizzes up close to me and says, "Get ready, Miss Daisy Dreamer. Because *this* is only the beginning!"

CHAPTER TWO

The Invitation Station

Posey and I sail out of the kitchen and into the Lollipop Garden. There are striped peppermint pops, twisty unicorn-horn pops, jumbo swirly pops, and bubble-gum pops. I pick a pink-and-green watermelon swirly pop.

We land on marshmallow chairs. They're not sticky, like in a s'more— just squishy, soft, and comfy.

"Do you know the first thing you'll need for your Daisy Dream Day?" Posey asks.

I slurp my lollipop. "That's easy!" I say. "We'll need one Daisy Dreamer!" *Obviously.*

Posey giggles. "Well, that's certainly true!" he says. "But you'll also need invitations to send to your guests!" Then Posey whips out a pad of paper. "Who would you like to invite?"

Of course I pick my best friends, Jasmine and Lily, first. And then I pick my grandmother Upsy next. I can't forget to invite her!

Then I list all the WOM friends I've made on my adventures with Posey. Pretty soon the list is long with names.

"This is fabulous, Daisy!" Posey says. "Now are you ready to pick your party invitations?"

I nod like crazy because I am very ready to pick my party invitations!

"Then let's head to the Invitation Station!" Posey says. "Shall we go by bus? Or by sleigh? Or perhaps on a scooter or skateboard? Maybe you'd like a dino-vertible?"

"What's a dino-vertible?" I ask.

"Hmm." He pauses. "I was hoping you'd know. I have no idea!"

Those are all good ways to get somewhere, I think. Except for the dino-vertible. It may be better to skip THAT magic ride. Then I have the best idea ever.

"What if we rode on . . . a magic carpet?" I ask.

Posey perks up, and with the snap of his fingers, a real magic carpet with pink hearts and pom-pom tassels appears out of nowhere.

"All aboard!" Posey announces.

I scramble onto the carpet. It's like sitting on a floaty cloud.

Posey climbs on after me and says, "Hang on!"

And—*shwoosh!*—we're off!

The Invitation Station is more like a train station. There are trains parked on different tracks.

We fly through the air and park by a sign that reads DAISY DREAMER. Hey, that's just like me!

Next to the trains are rows and rows of party invitations.

They have every card imaginable! Sparkly royal princess cards! Golden unicorn cards! Glittery mermaid cards! Ballerinas! Puppy dogs! Kittens! They're all completely adorable. *Obviously.*

"Do you see your perfect invitation?" Posey asks.

And that's when I find it! The card is shaped like a golden palace, and it's made of *real* gold paper! When I  pick up the card, it trumpets! Then the palace door opens all by itself, and a tiny teddy bear butler announces the details of my party.

"Hear ye, hear ye," the little bear says. "You are invited to the fantastically magical Daisy Dream Day!"

Posey hops from one foot to the other.

"That's a *bear-y* good choice!" he says.

We take the card to the front counter, where a fairy waves her wand over my invitation and guest list.

POOF! Fairy dust bursts into the air like mini fireworks, and the fairy smiles sweetly.

"Your invitations are ready to be delivered!" she says. Then she points to the door. "And your train is waiting!"

We hurry onto the platform and board the train. Instead of a whistle, I hear a familiar voice calling my name from far away.

"Daaaay-zeee! Daisy Dreamer . . ."

☆ CHAPTER THREE ☆

Ditsy Dreamer

"Knock, knock!" Mom says.

"Who's there?" I answer from under my covers, because it's morning and I'm still in bed.

"Who," Mom says.

"Who *who*?" I moan.

Mom laughs and answers, "Are you an *owl*?!"

I roll over in bed.

"As a matter of fact, I *am* an owl,"
I say. "And don't you know owls *sleep*
during the day?"

Then my dad comes in and tickles
my toes.

"Wake up, Daisy Dreamer!" he
says. "Or you'll dream the day away!"

I try to hide my toes, but it's no use.

"Okay, you win!" I giggle. "I'll get up."

Then I remember today is my Daisy Dream Day. *Or is it?* I wonder. Because I'm not in the WOM anymore.

I hop out of bed and drag my blanket with me, like I always do. My blanket is a magical robe that makes me invisible. But oh no! Sir Pounce, my secret spy pet cat, has found me again. And now he's sunk his claws into my robe.

"Let go!" I shout. "Or you'll snag my robe!"

I yank my blanket away, and *I* fall face-first onto the floor! *SPLAT!* Okay, I'm definitely awake now. *Obviously.*

I hop up and swirl my blanket around me like a fancy evening dress. Time to make my grand entrance.

I glide through the house like an enchanted princess . . . until my foot gets stuck in the blanket!

I crumple into a pile and wonder if something like that would happen on Dream Day. Probably not.

I leave my blanket in a heap and head for the kitchen. It's time for Toasty Squares!

But when I shake the cereal box over my bowl, nothing comes out. My Toasty Squares are all gone.

Oh no! That means only one thing. I have to eat my parents' cereal for breakfast: oat flakes with flaxseed oil.

I open the *Dreamer Report* to take my mind off things. The *Dreamer Report* is my very own newspaper, written by me.

But then, *oopsy-daisy!*

My elbow bumps my cereal bowl, and milk sloshes onto my *Dreamer Report.* Ink smears all over the place, and my stories are ruined.

Mom runs over with paper towels.
"Don't worry!" she says, mopping it
up. "I'll help you write a new *Dreamer
Report* after school."

I sigh loudly. *Am I Daisy Dreamer today?* I ask myself. Because I feel more like *Ditsy* Dreamer.

"Well, at least I still get to have my favorite lunch—homemade avocado sushi rolls," I say.

Then Mom gives Dad a weird look.

"Oh boy. I am *so* sorry, Daisy," Dad confesses. "I ate the last avocado before bed. . . ."

Wow! I think as I sit there, stunned. This is *not* how I pictured my Daisy Dream Day at all.

☆ CHAPTER FOUR ☆

Just a Dream

Clickety-clackety-clickety-clack!

I whiz down the sidewalk on my skateboard. Mom and I are both on our way to school—because my mom teaches there. She's *way* behind me, as usual. As I ride, I look everywhere for Posey because I really want my Daisy Dream Day to come true.

Then I hit a crack in the sidewalk.

Uh-oh, I'm going down.

Ka-bonkity bonk-bonk-bonk!

I end up flat on my stomach. Luckily, I land on the grass by the sidewalk.

"Daisy! Are you okay?" says someone.

I look up and see Gabby Gaburp
and her sidekick, Carol Rattinger.
Gabby offers me a hand and pulls
me up. Carol picks up my skateboard.
Sometimes these not-so-nice girls can
actually be pretty nice.

I check myself over. All I have are grass stains. Everywhere.

"I'm okay."

Carol hands me my skateboard.

"Well, that's good!" Gabby says. Then she hands me an envelope with my name on it.

"Would you like to come to my *half* birthday party tomorrow?" she asks. "I always have a half birthday party to practice for my *real* one."

I'm speechless, because number one:
Only Gabby would get two birthday
parties in a year. And number two:
She actually invited me!

"Sure thing," I say, because I would never turn down a party. *Obviously*.

Then Gabby and Carol skip toward school to hand out more invitations.

This makes me stop and wonder about my own party. Maybe Dream Day was just a dream.

At recess Lily, Jasmine, and I meet in the Hideout, which is under the slide. We have to crawl through a tunnel to get to it.

Once inside, I tell my friends about my dream and how it felt so real.

My friends laugh.

"You should write your dream in your journal," Jasmine suggests. "You know, the one your grandmother gave to you."

I feel my eyebrows shoot straight up. I forgot all about my journal. It's been sitting in the bottom of my backpack for weeks. I grab my backpack and dig in.

"Found it!" I hold the journal so my friends can see. "This is where I invented Posey in the first place!"

My friends giggle.

"Duh, Daisy!" Lily says. "We know! We've been making up stories about Posey for a long time now."

Jasmine nods, but I just stare at my friends.

What did they just say? That we MAKE UP the Posey stories?

CHAPTER FIVE

Posey Stories

I flip through the pages of my journal. There are so many Posey adventures! All of them begin with a story starter written by my grandmother Upsy. There are even pictures to go with each story.

"Do you want to read some, Daisy?" Lily asks.

"Yeah, go for it!" Jasmine says.

I open to the story about the snow day and read the story starter. *"What would you do with your imaginary friend on a snow day?"* Then I whisper, "That was the day Posey and I went bed-sledding."

Jasmine and Lily suddenly look confused.

"Oh, right. You weren't there," I remind them. "A bed-sled is a bed that can sled. Posey and I bed-sledded all over the WOM! We met the Snow-nimals—critters made of *snow*. Then we visited an ice castle and met a yeti named Naklin. We also had a giant snow-berang fight. *Zing! Splat! Poof!*"

Before my friends can say anything, I flip through the pages until I find the story starter that reads, *"What would happen if your imaginary friend went to the beach with you?"*

I laugh, because so much can happen when you take your imaginary friend to the beach!

"This!" I point to the page in the book. "This was the day Posey and I went to the beach and my cat, Sir Pounce, snuck along!

Then Posey turned me into a mermaid and turned Sir Pounce into a fish so we could travel underwater. We met a lost octopus named Inky and a whale named Humpfrey, and we found buried treasure!"

Jasmine and Lily just sit there, and I realize that I should remind them about one of their adventures with Posey.

"Okay, *this* one is for you! It's a doozy." I read the story starter, "'*What if your imaginary friend decides to go to school with you for a day?*'"

Now my friends laugh.

"I love this story!" Lily says. "It's about Posey stowing away in your backpack."

I nod wildly. "It was a total disaster! Remember when the bag of glitter-litter exploded *all* over me?!"

Lily laughs. "And then Posey's WOA friends took over the cafeteria and the playground!"

Jasmine shakes her head. "No, it's the WOM! World of Make-Believe."

"Oh yeah, sorry," says Lily. "It's hard to keep track of all these *made-up names.*"

My mouth drops open because I am shocked! These names are *not* made up!

Jasmine sees my reaction and quickly changes the subject. "Anyway, are you guys going to Gabby's half birthday?"

"Definitely!" Lily says.

But I'm stuck shaking my head because I'm *so* mixed up. *Of course these stories are real! And Posey and all his friends are real too . . . right?*

Chapter Six

Spin-and-Dare

"Daisy!" Mom calls after dinner. "I need your help! Upsy's coming to visit this weekend, and the house is a mess."

I run downstairs and look around. Mom's right. The house *is* a mess. There are board games out, playing cards on the floor, and two falling-down blanket forts in the middle of the family room.

"My friend Posey could clean up this mess in a *snap*," I say. "But he's not around."

Mom laughs. "Well, luckily, I have you and Dad!"

We each get to work. I pick up my games, fold the blankets, and play fifty-two-card pickup . . . by picking up all the cards. Dad empties the wastebaskets. Mom does the dinner dishes. Then we dust and vacuum, and before long I am wiped-out tired!

With a huge yawn and a stretch, I barely make it to bed before I fall totally asleep.

The next day is the most normal day ever. Nothing magic happens at all, but I don't mind. Some days are like that, I guess. It makes the magic days even more magic.

After school Lily, Jasmine, and I go to Gabby's party. Every kid I know is there!

"Daisy!" Gabby cheers. "You came! Come over and play. We're playing Spin-and-Dare."

I know this game. Players sit in a circle with a bottle in the middle. One person spins the bottle, and if it points to you when it stops, then you have to pick a dare from a basket. If you don't perform the dare, you're O-U-T out. *Obviously.*

"The winner gets a gift card to Icing on the Cake!" Gabby announces. Icing on the Cake happens to be the best bakery around.

"Oooooooh!" we all exclaim. Then Gabby spins the bottle, and it lands on me!

I dig for a dare and read it out loud. "'I dare you to tell a story.'"

Lily and Jasmine squeal because they know I love to tell stories.

"Okay, here goes," I begin. "One day Jasmine, Lily, and I were playing at the park with our magical friend, Posey. Jasmine's basketball flew over the fence, and we found it by the old well."

Gabby bounces up and down. "I know that well!"

I nod and continue.

"But did you know that it was a wishing well? Yeah, it was broken, and Posey fixed it by putting a missing stone back in place. And you'll never guess what happened next."

Everybody's eyes grew wide, and they leaned in closer. I had them hooked!

"All the ungranted wishes inside the well"—I paused for effect—"were *granted*! Hundreds of wishes all came true *at the same time*. My mom got the pony she wished for when she was a little girl. And Gabby turned into a fairy-tale princess!"

Gabby smiles. "That was my wish from the well! But how did *you* know that?"

"Um, lucky guess?" I suggest, and all the guests laugh.

"What about me?" asks Carol. "Can you guess my wish from the well?"

"Sure," I say. "You wished you could talk to animals."

"How . . . ," she says with a giggle. "How could you know that?"

"Everyone knows that," admits Gabby. "You tell it to anyone who will listen."

Then I shrug and wrinkle my nose. "But there was a teensy problem with your wish, Carol," I add.

"There was once a pack of squirrels that found out that you could talk to animals, and they had *tons* of questions to ask you," I told her. "Be careful what you wish for, I guess."

The room shrieks with laughter. Then I turn to John Gates.

"It wasn't just Carol. John, you wished you could fly, but then you couldn't get back on the ground! And Wren Sinclair wished for a million cats, but that meant she had to clean up *after* a million cats."

Wren covers her mouth with her hand, and the rest of the kids fall on one another with laughter.

"So you see," I go on, "the wishes made everything out of control. Posey tried to reverse the wishes, but he only made them more powerful."

Everyone's eyes are fixed on me.

"What happened next, Daisy?" Gabby asks, looking a little scared.

"Luckily, there was only one person in the whole town who had *never* made a wish at the well," I say.

"WHO?" the group asks.

"Me," I say with a smile. "I flipped a coin into the well and wished for everything to go back to normal. And—*sha-zing!*—all the wishes disappeared and the madness stopped! The end!"

All the guests clap for my story. And suddenly the day feels magic again.

☆ Chapter Seven ☆

Surprise!

I wake up the next morning and feel like I've been dreaming for days. What if I have? What if this was all a dream?

I jump out of bed and grab an erasable marker from my desk. Then I draw a door on the wall—right next to my bedroom door.

Squeak! Squeak! Squeak!

I knock on my freshly drawn door.

Posey almost always answers when I knock on a drawn door.

Sir Pounce watches and waits too. I knock again, louder this time. I put my ear to the door and . . . I hear *footsteps*.

"Daisy?" a voice calls out. "Daisy Dreamer!"

A door opens, but it's not my hand-drawn door. It's my bedroom door. My grandmother peeks inside.

"I didn't mean to wake you," Upsy says. "Since you are up, I'd love to take you out for breakfast."

The word "breakfast" makes my stomach growl out loud, which makes Upsy and me both laugh.

"Of course!" I say. "I'd love to have breakfast with you, Upsy! Let me get changed."

As I run to my dresser, I take one last peek at the door on the wall. There's still no sign of Posey.

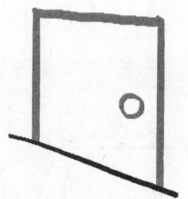

Then I realize something new. Maybe Upsy will have an answer!

CHAPTER EIGHT

The Letter

Upsy takes me to my favorite breakfast spot—the Flapjack Shack. I order a sticky stack of chocolate chip pancakes. I poke at my pancakes with my fork. I'm hungry, but I don't feel like eating.

"What's the matter, Daisy?"

I sip my water.

"Oh, nothing . . . ," I say.

Upsy rests her hand on my arm. "I can tell something's wrong. And maybe I can help."

I sigh.

"Okay," I begin. "The trouble is my imaginary friend, Posey. He's gone missing. We used to have adventures together all the time. He was even planning a special Daisy Dream Day for me. But now I'm beginning to think Posey is all in my imagination, and I'm all mixed up."

Upsy gets very quiet, but I can tell she's trying to figure out what to say. She probably thinks I'm being silly, like a little kid, so I try to erase what I said.

"Never mind, Upsy," I tell her. "I mean, all this make-believe stuff is so babyish. Forget I said anything."

But Upsy shakes her head.

"It's not babyish, Daisy," she says. "Imaginations make the impossible possible. Once upon a time, people only imagined flying like birds, and then they invented airplanes. People also dreamed about going to the moon, and then they really walked on the moon!"

Next Upsy pulls a piece of paper
from her purse.

"Do you remember this letter?" she
asks, handing it to me.

"Of course I remember it," I say.
"I'm the one who wrote it!"

I had written Upsy a letter and given her a story starter when I was trying to help a new friend in the World of Make-Believe. The story starter was *There once was a magical friend named Sweetheart. . . .*

On the back of the letter I made a dot-to-dot drawing of the Sparkle Fairy.

I hold up the letter.

"Posey was the one who delivered this letter to you!" I say. "This is proof that my Posey adventures were real!"

"Well, *almost* real," Upsy says with a wink. "Now it's time to wake up, Miss Daisy Dreamer!"

Chapter Nine ☆

Rise and Shine

And then I *do* wake up. I'm in my own bed. But wait . . . I'm *not* in my own room. And I'm *not* alone!

"Is that you, Sir Pounce?" I call.

Then I see my beloved purple friend.

"Nope. It's me!" he cheers.

"POSEY!" I shout. "It's SO good to see you!"

Posey smiles and then turns away.

"Hey, everyone! Look!" he shouts. "Daisy's awake! Let's get this Dream Day started!"

Posey bounces over and pulls me out of bed.

"Come on, Daisy Dreamer! I have something to show you!"

Posey leads me to a giant playroom. Twinkly lights dot the ceiling like starry gems. I see indoor swings, a dance floor, and a live band. There are round tables with party hats, noisemakers, and bouquets of lighted balloons.

But best of all, I see everyone I invited to my party! There's Jasmine and her lost-and-now-found Imaginary, KitCat. And there's Lily and Upsy with their Sparkle Fairies! And I see Pretty Pixies! Hot-Toppers! Snow-nimals! And Naklin, my yeti friend.

Then Posey jumps onto the stage and grabs the microphone.

"Welcome to Daisy's Dream Day! Daisy has a spectacular imagination. She is not only part of what makes the WOM magical—she makes it *real* for everyone. Thanks, Daisy. Now let's get this party started!"

Then everyone cheers! And I cheer too because who doesn't like a party with all your friends—real *and* imaginary?! *Obviously.*

This is truly a Daisy Dream come true.

Chapter Ten

The Real Deal

I try a little bit of *everything*. I have a Daisy Dreamsicle, which is an orange Popsicle with vanilla-cream daisies. I take one sticky bite of a caramel apple, two nibbles of a popcorn ball, and two huge chomp-er-oos of one of my fizzy cupcakes. Then I offer treats to all my friends! Once we've eaten, it's time for the games to begin!

Now I'm ready to *motor*. I play glow-in-the-dark hopscotch games with Jasmine. I hop on the indoor swings with Lily. And I boogie on the dance floor with all my WOM friends.

Then Posey waves for me to follow him outside.

"How do you like your Daisy Dream Day?" Posey asks.

I lean back and sigh happily. "It's the dreamiest," I say.

The World of Make-Believe stretches out before us. It sparkles with colors that I can't even describe. Cloud Critters wave to us as they float through the sky.

It's almost too good to be true.

"Posey, I had a really bad dream this week—*or, at least, I think it was a dream*," I begin. "I dreamed that you were just in my imagination. That none of our adventures were real."

Posey smiles warmly and says, "Daisy, don't you know . . . your imagination is one-hundred-percent real! Everyone's imagination is real. Our imagination is what makes us special. It makes us one of a kind."

Then Posey points to the valleys, lakes, and mountains beyond.

"Just look, Daisy! This is your World of Make-Believe!" he cries. "There are millions of others, but this one is yours!

We can go wherever we want! We can meet whoever we'd like! So where do you want to dream next?"

I feel a huge smile bloom on my face. I reach out and grab Posey's hand.

"Anywhere," I say. "So long as I'm with *you*."

And suddenly I know in my heart that Posey and the WOM *are* real because they are a part of me. And they will always be a part of me . . .

. . . no matter how grown-up I get.

Read a
little dream . . .
with Daisy Dreamer!

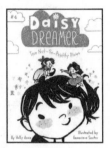